A
Midnight Clear

Merry Christmas 2003
Brandon !
♡ Mom + Dad

A
Midnight Clear

Selected
Family Christmas Stories

KATHERINE PATERSON

SCHOLASTIC INC.

New York Toronto London Auckland Sydney
Mexico City New Delhi Hong Kong Buenos Aires

ISBN 0-439-63249-8

12 11 10 9 8 7 6 5 4 3 2 1   3 4 5 6 7 8/0

Printed in the U.S.A.   40

First Scholastic printing, December 2003

for all the saints
of
Lafayette Presbyterian Church
Norfolk, Virginia
and
First Presbyterian Church
Barre, Vermont
with gratitude and love

Still through the cloven skies they come,
With peaceful wings unfurled;
And still their heavenly music floats
O'er all the weary world;
Above its sad and lowly plains
They bend on hovering wing:
And ever o'er its Babel sounds
The blessed angels sing.

"It Came Upon the Midnight Clear"
Edmund Hamilton Sears, 1810–1876

Contents

A Midnight Clear

✳

Merit Badges

"SCOUTS," Mrs. Bushey was saying, "we are entirely too involved in ourselves." It was all I could do to keep from snickering out loud. I didn't dare look at Amy. We'd both collapse. Mrs. Bushey always said "scouts," not "girls" or "kids" like a normal grown-up, or "students" like a teacher.

How did the woman ever get to be a scout leader, anyhow? I wondered. Well, of course, Judy quit to have a baby. That's how. They were desperate for somebody—anybody—to take over. But where would you dig up someone like Bushey? All of us called her Bushey behind her back. It absolutely fit. She had a bad home permanent that frizzed all over her strange little round head and she never shaved her legs. She was a sight.

"What?" I hadn't been paying attention. Apparently, Bushey had been plowing ahead with some harebrained scheme (no pun intended).

"Are we agreed then, Scout Hensen?"

"Sure, okay." What in the world had I agreed to do? I'd have to ask Amy afterward.

"Then here are the names of the residents and a little bit about each. We won't be able to make special friends with every one. We just wouldn't have the time, what with our busy school and activity schedules, would we?" Why did Bushey always say "we"? Didn't the woman know any other pronouns? *Residents?* I suddenly heard the word. What was Bushey talking about? What residents?

"There," said Bushey happily, "we have made a start in caring. We scouts must endeavor to be caring persons, mustn't we?"

The ten of us somehow got through Bushey's closing ceremony of the scout pledge and a song about friendship that must have been written about the time of the *Mayflower*.

We stumbled out of the dark church basement into

the late afternoon sunshine. But not before every other member of the troop was looking at me, their smirks exploding into shrieks. "Ah-ha, Kate, Bushwhacked, Bushwhacked." Amy had made up that term for anyone in the troop who let Bushey sucker her into something.

"What do you mean? I didn't get Bushwhacked. I wanted to."

"You're lying." Amy stared at me.

Now I was caught. I couldn't admit that I had no idea what I'd promised to do.

"Kate! You know perfectly well what happened when Judy took us there last Christmas."

"Christmas?" Here was a clue.

"The caroling. The 'disaster of the decade!' " That's what Judy had called our attempt to cheer up the residents at Logan Manor. My skin began to creep. Had I promised to do something at the manor? "That was just one crazy old woman," I said nervously.

"Sto—op!" Amy yelled. "Stop the noise!" imitating the old woman who had raced out of her room while we were singing "Silent Night." We'd been scared silly at the time, but now it was one of our group jokes. Whenever we wanted to make each other giggle, somebody would began imitating the old lady who had driven us out of the nursing home where we had gone to carol last Christmas.

All the others joined in. "Sto—op! Stop the noise!"

"So?" I pretended not to care. "She's not the only person there. I don't have to try to cheer *her* up. I can choose someone else."

"Aren't we a *good* scout?" Laura pinched her mouth in a perfect imitation of Bushey. "Shut up, Laura," I muttered. I could just see Bushey's frizzed head coming up the steps out of the basement.

It was bedtime before I looked at the list that Bushey had given me. It was typed, but obviously by someone who could barely do so. There were twenty-six names on the list. All women. All old. There were stars beside about ten of the names. At the bottom it said: "★These residents have no one who comes to visit on a regular basis." There were four names that had double stars. "★★These residents have no visitors."

Suddenly I felt freezing cold. I put on my bathrobe and went downstairs. My mother was still in the kitchen packing lunches for the next day. "Mom?"

"Katie. I thought you were already in bed."

"I'm just going."

She looked at me for a minute. "Is something the matter?"

"No." I felt silly and about four years old. "I guess—I guess I just wanted to come down and make sure you were here," I said.

She smiled. "Where else would I be, Pumpkin?" It was a baby name she hardly ever used anymore.

I kissed her cheek. "I love you, Mom."

"I love you, too. Now off to bed with you."

IT WAS A couple of days before I looked at the list again. By this time I'd decided several things. One, I would not choose anyone who *never* had visitors. That was likely to get me the stop-the-noise crazy one in that bunch. If I was going to do this—and none of my friends believed for a minute that I had the nerve—I would have to choose someone who wouldn't run me off or scare me to death.

On the other hand, it didn't seem quite fair to choose someone who already had regular visitors. That left the ten one-starred residents. The ones on this list with scary descriptions like "probable Alzheimer's" or "unable to speak" or "deaf" I crossed off. We were a scout, not a doctor or a psychologist, right? We were not going to bite off more than we could chew and give our friends the satisfaction of seeing us fail.

This got the list down to three residents. I chose Mildred Hull (husband deceased, no children, likes to play cards) because if you couldn't think of anything to say, you could always play cards. And besides, if the woman could play cards, she couldn't be totally off her rocker.

Monday afternoon was scout meeting. I was determined to make my first visit before then, but Sunday came and I still hadn't gone. I was tempted to ask Mom to go with me. But she and Dad had promised to do something at church. I dragged out my scout uniform, which had been in the closet since the "disaster of the decade." The sleeves cut me under the arms, and I looked really doofy. But I told myself it was like wearing a costume for Halloween. You could be someone else dressed up. I guess I needed the protection.

At the desk near the front door was a very skinny woman with an enormous head of hair that made her look lopsided. I bit the inside of my cheek to keep from giggling.

"Yes, honey?" the woman said. She didn't look like the kind of woman that would call you honey, but never mind. I cleared my throat. "I'm here to see Mrs. Hull," I said.

"Who?"

"Mrs. Mildred Hull." From barely a croak I went to a boom, and the woman ducked her head as if to say, "They're deaf, not me."

But all she said was: "Is Mildred expecting you?"

"Oh." I should have called. It was a little late to think of that now. "I don't think so. I'm Kathryn Hensen—I'm—from the Girl Scouts."

"Where is your leader?" That's what the aliens always want to know. I shrugged. Let her think my leader forgot or something.

She considered me. "Well," she said finally, "why don't you wait here while I go and see what Mildred's up to. A lot of our little people like to take a nap in the afternoon." Her voice dropped to a whisper as though she was letting me in on a big secret.

There was nothing to do but stand there by the desk while old women shuffled past, staring me up and down as if I was an endangered species in the zoo. The label of my uniform scratched the back of my neck, and I could feel the seams cutting the flesh under my arms. I should have worn something comfortable. But it was too late now.

Finally, the receptionist came trotting back. "This is Mildred," she said.

I was buffaloed. The receptionist was standing there all alone. For a minute I thought one of her "little people" was invisible, and then I realized that, clumping slowly up the long corridor behind a walker, was an old, old woman who must be Mildred Hull (husband deceased, no children).

I didn't know whether to run down the hall and stop the poor old thing from making the torturous trip all the way to the front desk or just to stand there and wait, trying not to stare.

"Mildred says she doesn't know you," said the receptionist as though to fill the time. "But some of our little people get confused."

Our little people? "No," I said. "No, she wouldn't have any way of knowing me."

"But wasn't your group here at Christmas, or was that some other—?"

"Uh, Mrs. Hull?" I double-stepped it down the hall toward the bent figure.

The white head twisted up, the arms leaning heavily on the metal frame. "Last time I checked," she said. "And you?"

"We—I'm Kate Hensen. I'm a Girl Scout." What were you supposed to say?

"Oh, I get it. I couldn't imagine why any young

girl I never heard of was coming to see me. I'm a merit badge."

"No. Really."

"Let me be a merit badge, please. I don't think I'm up to being a good deed for the day."

I guess I just stood there with my mouth open.

"If it's any comfort, our uniforms were worse. Lots worse." I tried to smile. "Well, if I can't get you a merit badge, what can I do for you?" she asked.

"Maybe we could sit down somewhere?"

"Sure. No stamina, you kids today. No stamina."

She clumped her way to the little sitting area near the front door. I followed her, my hands out ready to catch the woman if she stumbled. I hovered around while the she heaved herself into a straight chair and then nodded at me to take the overstuffed one next to it.

"Tell me about yourself," the old woman said, after she had caught her breath from the trip down the hall. "I haven't seen a live child close-up for ages. What are you like?"

"Like? Me?"

"Yeah. What would you be doing for example if you hadn't been shamed into coming to visit some poor little old lady today?"

"I— What?"

"Oh, come on now Kathryn or Kitty or—?"

"Kate. Everyone calls me Kate."

"Is that what you want to be called?"

"Well, yeah, I guess so."

"I like to call people what they want to be called." She lowered her voice and leaned toward me. "Stick, there," she whispered, jerking her head toward the receptionist, "calls me Mildred. I hate it."

"Stick?"

"Yeah, shhhh. We call her that because she looks like those stick figures little kids draw. You know."

I giggled out loud. I couldn't help myself.

"All these young aides here call me Mildred, too. I hate it. No one in my life ever called me Mildred."

"What do you want to be called?"

"My friends used to call me Millie." She leaned toward me again. "Promise you won't tell?"

I nodded, even though I had no idea what I was promising.

"My older brother used to call me Mildew."

"Mildew?" I looked at the woman, trying to see a little girl with a brother who called her Mildew. It was hard to imagine.

"For years, I burst into tears every time he said it," she said. "Silly, huh?"

"My brother used to call me Spook," I said.

"Spook?"

"My birthday is on Halloween. I hated that nickname. My mom calls me Pumpkin sometimes, and I don't mind at all."

"It's the way she says it, right?" She was quiet for a minute. "Ralph was my brother's friend. I was seventeen when I met him, and let me tell you the minute I saw that man I knew I wanted to marry him. When my brother introduced me as his sister, 'Mildew,' I was ready to kill him." She shook her head. "You know what Ralph called me till the day he died? Dewy." She gave her head a little shake. "Dewy. I thought it was the most beautiful name a girl could ever have."

I stared at her face hidden by thick, smudged glasses, trying hard to see that teenage girl so crazy with love. Then I realized Mrs. Hull was staring back and I said quickly, "Would you like to play some cards?"

"Cards? Why would I want to play cards? I hate cards."

"The, uh—" How could you tell a person they were on a list (husband deceased, no children)? "They—uh—told me you liked to play cards."

"I play cards. Sure. With people who can't make conversation. Why should I play with you?" She cocked her head. "I guess we scare kids, don't we, with our white heads and false teeth and all our handicaps and infirmities. Yeah, I guess that's it. We're like monsters, aren't we, to healthy children like you."

"No," I said, "really." But I felt a tingle as I said it.

"I thought we'd never see anyone under the age of fifty in here again after last Christmas."

"Last Christmas?"

"A bunch of kids—Girl Scouts, too. I remember the uniforms. They came in here all brave and shiny to give the poor old coots some holiday cheer—" She started to giggle. "You're not going to believe this—"

Try me.

"My roommate. She's a harmless old soul, but they woke her out of a sound sleep. And right in the middle of these little girls sweetly chirping away, she comes roaring out of the room screaming her head off. Those little green girls ran like Frankenstein himself was upon them." She started to laugh. "I'm sorry," she said, "it does seem mean to laugh, but it was the funniest sight we've had around here since Stick got her new hairdo. We'll never forget that night." She looked at me sharply. "You think we're cruel? Getting so much fun at the expense of those poor scared children?"

I shook my head. "Someday they will probably look back on it and laugh," I said.

"We take our fun where we can get it around here," she said, almost as if apologizing. "I really don't approve of making fun of people"—she jerked her head toward the receptionist—"with perhaps the one major exception. I used to say to my daughter, June, I'd say—"

Daughter?

"What's the matter? Oh. If I have a daughter, why am I here? Or why doesn't she come to see me? Is that it?"

"Well, they said—"

"She's dead."

What were you supposed to say to something like that? I opened my mouth, but there were no words.

"It was a long time ago. But it's hard, you know. No, of course you don't know. You're what? Ten? Eleven?"

"Almost twelve."

"I hope you never know. I thought when Ralph died I would never get over it, but losing your child —having your beautiful child die— Why should I be the one to live on and on?" she asked angrily. "What is my life worth? It isn't right," she said more quietly. "It's just not right." She fumbled around in the sleeve of the old housedress she was wearing. "Excuse me," she said. "This is embarrassing, but when I left my room, I didn't seem to bring a tissue."

I rooted in my pocket and pulled out a very wrinkled Kleenex. Mrs. Hull took off the thick glasses and wiped her eyes. "Thank you," she said. "You can mention that for the merit badge. Always be prepared. Or something like that. Don't tell them it was used. They may take off points."

"WE DON'T SUPPOSE we have anything to report about our project at Logan Manor?" Bushey looked wistful, like a kid asking Santa for a toy that she knew she wasn't going to get.

"I went Sunday afternoon," I said. The rest of the troop turned in their chairs to stare, but Bushey was smiling. She had a nice smile. She ought to smile more often.

"Yeah, I went through the list and picked a person they said didn't have any regular visitors. I didn't want to be running competition to somebody's darling grandchild."

"Did you get—you know who?" Laura whispered loudly.

"Who?" asked Bushey.

"This woman we met when we were caroling last year. No," I said to the others, "I was pretty careful about that." They laughed nervously.

"And?"

"Her name was Mrs. Hull and she said she didn't want to be my merit badge"—I ignored the noises the others were making—"but that she'd rather be a merit badge than a good deed."

"Which was she?" Amy asked.

"Neither. I liked her. I think she likes me, too. I'm going back to see her next week."

But Tuesday night Bushey called. The receptionist had made a mistake. Unaccompanied minors were not allowed to visit residents. "We could go with you," Bushey said.

"No!" As soon as I yelled it, I was sorry. "It's not you, Mrs. Bushey, it's the principle of the thing. I'm not going to misbehave. And I'm not going to give her some disease. I just want to talk with her. It wouldn't be the same with another person listening over our shoulders."

"If you're not comfortable with us, your mother might—"

"No, Mrs. Bushey, it's not you, really. I don't want my mother, either. I don't want to have to be baby-sat when I'm visiting with a friend."

"We understand," Bushey said, "and we think you're absolutely right. We will call the owner."

"Thanks, Bushey," I said, not even realizing that I'd forgotten the "Mrs.," "but I think Mrs. Hull and I can handle this."

"May we say how proud we are, Scout Hensen?"

"Sure," I said.

I called Logan Manor immediately, but the night person told me that it was too late for calls. "It's only eight," I said.

"Our little people need their rest." Apparently the night person was a Stick clone.

The next afternoon, they let me talk to Mrs. Hull who was, as I was sure she would be, outraged.

"You come over here and we'll give that Mervin Wertz a piece of your mind. At my age, I don't have any to spare. And don't wear your uniform. Wear something that fits and makes you look like your parents could buy this place out and have money left over to burn."

When I arrived, dressed in the suit that my grandmother had sent me for Easter, Stick was on duty. I even wore my only pair of panty hose. I had started to sneak some of Mom's makeup, but I was afraid she'd make a fuss.

"Oh yes, Kathy, isn't it?" Stick was rigid (pun intended).

"Kate Hensen. I think Mrs. Hull made an appointment for the two of us to speak to Mr. Wertz."

"Mildred and Gracie are already in his office," she said.

I opened the door. A man, a shriveled little man, was seated behind an enormous desk. Standing in front of him was Mrs. Hull, leaning on her walker with one hand and pounding on it with the other. In a chair on the opposite side of the room sat the person who Stick called Gracie, better known to me as "Stop-the-Noise." My blood froze, but I went into the room.

Mrs. Hull was saying something that ended with ". . . the Constitution of the United States of America."

Mr. Wertz was getting very small and very pale. Everyone turned to look at me. I was glad I'd dressed so carefully.

"Is this the child?" Mr. Wertz asked.

"She has a name!" Mrs. Hull shouted. "She has a name. She is a person!"

"Kate Hensen," I said. "How do you do, Mr. Wertz?" I walked over and offered him my hand. I was so polite and mature my grandmother would have fainted with joy.

Mr. Wertz ignored my hand. "It's very sweet of you little girls to want to cheer up our residents" (at least he didn't say "little people"), "but this is a medical and nursing facility, not a day care center." He smiled. I guess he thought it was a little joke. "We have some residents"—he gave Gracie a nervous glance—"who may be upset by unsupervised young visitors. And well, sometimes children are upset by elderly residents who, well, how shall I put it—?"

"Shut up!" Stop-the-Noise had jumped to her feet.

"As you see—"

"Shut up, I said!"

Mr. Wertz blinked rapidly. "Well, I don't really feel that we need to discuss this further. Our Gracie—"

"I'm not your Gracie!"

Mr. Wertz must have rung a bell or something because a young woman in a white uniform was there almost immediately. She took Gracie, or whatever Mrs. Hull's roommate was really named, by the arm and led her out of the room, shutting the door behind them. I could hear the old woman shouting down the hall as she went.

"You see, my dear, little children"—again my grandmother would have been proud that I didn't correct him—"sometimes, without even meaning to, can have an upsetting effect."

"Mr. Wertz, excuse me, but I think she was upset by you, not by me."

"She's right," Mrs. Hull said. "Mrs. Ticknor hates being called Gracie."

"We always call our people by their first names," Mr. Wertz said.

"I know," said Mrs. Hull, "and some of us always hate it."

I left that one alone. "Mr. Wertz," I said, "Mrs. Hull and I are friends—not close friends, I admit. We haven't had time for that. But we'd like to get to know each other better. We can't do that with chaperons. Frankly, we find the idea insulting. We are both perfectly intelligent people. I promise you that if you will allow me to come and visit Mrs. Hull, you will not regret it." I tried to put into my voice a hint that my family had untold millions, some of which would surely be donated to his nursing home if he agreed, but I can't be sure all that came through.

"And if it's any comfort to you, Mr. Wertz," said Mrs. Hull, "I will try to behave just as beautifully as my friend here."

"Whew," she said as we escaped after our triumph to a private corner of the lounge. "That was a near thing."

"Yeah," I said. "What's-her-name, Gracie, I mean—"

"Mrs. Ticknor to you," Mrs. Hull said. "Yeah, great, wasn't she?"

"What?"

"Yeah, right on cue. We couldn't have done it without her. Remind me to pick up a Hershey bar for her. Kind of our merit badge system. You know how it goes."

"I'm learning," I said.

BUSHEY AND I dragged the whole troop over to Logan Manor at Christmastime. Not to carol. Mrs. Hull vetoed that. We had a sing with the residents. Bushey, to my amazement, plays a mean piano, and Stick, when she unbends a bit, has a nice alto voice. Stick and I passed out songbooks, and the Girl Scouts scattered among the crowd. Gracie, I mean Mrs. Ticknor, mostly listened quietly, but when we got to "Joy to the World," I could hear her off-key "repeat the sounding joy" over and over long after the rest of us had gone on to the third verse. I smiled at Mrs. Hull, who smiled at me, and then Stick, who smiled at both of us. We all smiled at Bushey, who had a smile as wide as the stripes on the flag. We were all joyful. I think it was the first time I really understood the meaning of the word.

Poor Little Innocent Lamb

ISAIAH HAD PITIED the child before he ever lay eyes on her. Anyone who had to come live with Old Lettie was to be pitied, but when he saw her climbing down off the Greyhound, the last step almost too much for her skinny little white legs, his heart went out to her as it did to one of his hurt and helpless creatures. They weren't his creatures, of course. It wasn't his farm. It was Old Lettie's farm, but she never went out the door of the farmhouse to tend to it. She just nursed the account books, as though numbers on paper were a farm. So although he was only the hired man, it was, in actual fact, his farm, and all the creatures were his to care for.

Except this one getting off the bus—this poor little girl, dark, stringy hair past her narrow shoulders, and deep, sad eyes. Her face was streaked with dirt—tears, he thought at the time, though later he wondered. The child never cried.

"So," he said, when he had settled her and her tiny vinyl suitcase into the cab of the pickup. "So—you Miss Lettie's grandniece, eh? I got a passel of grand-nieces and -nephews myself."

There was no answer. Maybe she wasn't at ease with black folks. He tried again. "I told you already my name's Isaiah, but you ain't told me your name."

She was kicking the seat rhythmically with the back of her legs, staring straight ahead.

"Look," he said, starting the motor and watching the rearview mirror as he backed carefully out of the Greyhound parking lot. "I'll tell you right off, it might be kinda lonely for you out on the farm. Miss Lettie don't go out, and the animals aren't big talkers. Now, I live over the garage and you may figure I'm just the hired help, but I expect I'll be the best company around. If you don't make friends with me, it's likely to be mighty lonesome for you."

She looked at him sideways, and, for a moment, stopped her kicking. "Travis," she said.

"Huh?"

"It's my name. Travis."

He didn't tell her he'd never heard of such a fool name for a little girl. But then, any mother fool enough to ship a baby like this off to live with the very aunt she'd run off from when she was a girl was likely to saddle her poor child with some crazy name. Isaiah thought of his own loving mother, who had given each of her eight children a name from the Bible so that they could grow up straight and proud. She still fussed over him as she had when he was tiny—and he sixty years old come February.

He thought of his sisters and brothers and nieces and nephews and all their children, tumbling in and out of one another's lives in noisy, happy confusion. He turned and smiled at this little deserted thing beside him to show that he didn't hold her name against her, but she kept staring straight ahead, even though she couldn't see over the dashboard, and never looked his way.

"Well," he said at last. "Here we are." He got out and opened the gate, drove through, and got out again to close it. They rattled up the graveled drive to the old farmhouse. It was a huge, white frame, which had been added to and taken away from for a hundred years or more until Old Lettie's father finally wrapped it around with porches and gingerbread trim, putting an end to all his ancestors' tinkering. Isaiah drove the pickup around to the back as usual. "You'd best go in at the front," he told the child as he leaned across her to open the door. "I'll bring your bag."

She climbed down and followed the direction of his head around the west porch and the pyracantha bushes to the front door. He got her bag. It was too light to hold anything worth having. Lucille should have sent some warm clothes with the child. Lord have mercy. He shook his head. Poor little innocent lamb.

She was waiting at the front door. "It's locked," she said.

"Nah, ain't locked. Just got to yank hard," he said, pulling the heavy door open for her. "I expect Miss Lettie's upstairs. Little sitting room at the top of the staircase . . ." That mean old thing. She could at least come down to welcome the poor little scared creature. She could've gone to the bus station if she'd had half an ounce of kindness about her.

All she did when she got the news was rant about how no 'count Lucille was and how no 'count Lucille's mother Mildred had been, and how her whole life was plagued with nothing but no 'count bums, including him, Isaiah Washington. He'd nearly taken off on the spot. The only thing that kept him around enduring her insults year after year was the animals. If he left, what would become of the poor creatures?

He followed the child, her sneakered feet dragging as she went down the long dark hall, past the huge mirrored coat-and-umbrella stand on the left, the mahogany table with the plastic flower arrangement on the right. She paused a second, just to touch the flowers, and then, clinging to the right side of the hallway, she made her way to the foot of the long staircase. She took a deep breath and started up, holding onto the banister as if to pull herself along. He stood below, waiting to hear what the old woman would say. At last the child crossed the threshold into the room.

"So you're Travis." The shrill angry voice traveled down the stairs. "What kind of a name is that supposed to be?" As though the child were to blame. As though the child, long before she was born, had made first her grandmother and then her mother run away from this house. As though the child had chosen to come here to torment the bitter old woman.

"You look like your mother. Same wild-looking eyes . . . Well, don't just stand there staring. Can't you see I'm busy? Some of us do our duty . . ."

He wanted to run and pick up that suitcase and whack that mean old face. Instead, he called to the child and took her downstairs to the tiny bedroom off the kitchen and put her little suitcase on the bed. There were bigger, grander rooms in the old house, but none that would be as warm. And he had known even before he saw her that she would need to have a warm little nest in this cold house. All winter he kept a fire going in the big iron stove. He would take care of her. Of all the creatures God had given him to tend, he pitied her the most.

IT WAS HE who took the child to town and bought her warm pants to cover her thin legs. It was he who enrolled her in the county school. If it rained, he always managed to be at the stop in the pickup when the bus door opened.

The child never thanked him. Not because she was rude, but because since that first day she hardly spoke at all. The house was as quiet with the child living in it as it had been with only the old woman. Isaiah did the cooking, as he had for years now, and sometimes Old Lettie would leave her account books and deign to come to the kitchen table. Most often she demanded that he bring the meal up to her. Her life had not been changed by the presence of the child.

The child seemed to sense that she was not to bother her grandaunt. She almost tiptoed about the house, and when they were at the table together, she was as silent as a doll baby, hardly eating for fear it might disturb. Sometimes, when she thought her aunt wasn't looking, she would stare at the old woman with her big, sorrowful eyes. It nearly broke Isaiah's heart to see.

He had never had any children of his own, but he was awash in grandnieces and -nephews. He spent his Sundays being crawled over by children. They were noisy, happy, naughty children, frisky as young lambs. It wasn't right, he knew, for a child of eight to be so quiet.

ONE DAY WHEN she was at school, he determined to speak to Old Lettie about it. She was the child's grandaunt, after all, whether she had chosen to be or not. He found her hunched over the account books in her little sitting room. The door was open, but he knocked anyway.

"What's the matter?" she snapped. "Haven't you got work to do?"

"Miss Lettie, I got to talk to you."

"Well, make it quick."

"That child's about to starve."

"Don't be ridiculous."

"She's starving for notice. If you'd just talk to her. Pay her a little mind."

"You pay a mind to your affairs, Isaiah, and leave me to pay a mind to mine. By the way, I hope you're remembering that the price you got for lamb last spring was twenty-five cents *less* than you got the year before. You'll have to do better than that."

"Yes ma'am," he said, determining that Travis would be his to pay mind to from then on. But he couldn't do it alone. "Lord," he prayed, "you got to help me save this baby girl."

He began to talk to her all the time she was about. It didn't matter that she didn't answer or didn't even seem to listen half the time. He was determined to talk her ear off. He hadn't realized how hard talking was. He often ran out of things to say and had to repeat himself. He told her Bible stories and stories about when he was a little boy. He even took to buying a newspaper when he went to town so he could talk to her about the news.

"And this man sold his business and they gave him a check for fifty-six thousand dollars to pay for it, and his dog *ate the check!*" The two of them were peeling potatoes. Travis didn't look up from her spud. He nudged her. "His dog ate the check right down. Now that check was for thousands. That's his whole life's work right down the gullet of his poodle. Now what was he gonna do? He calls up the bank and says: 'My dog done ate up my check. Would you kindly write me another one?' 'Course they think the fellow is crazy in the head or trying to cheat 'em, one or the other. So they say he got to bring proof. Well, ain't but one way to bring proof . . .'"

Suddenly he realized that he'd gotten himself further into the story than he'd meant to. After all, she was just a little girl. He cleared his throat. "Well, I guess you wouldn't want to know about that . . ."

"I swallowed a nickel once." Her solemn voice was hardly louder than a whisper.

"Sure enough?"

"Yeah," she said. "The doctor at the clinic said you just have to wait."

"That's right. That's just what the man had to do."

Had he imagined it, or had she actually smiled at her potato?

IT WAS LATE November when he realized that the Lord was answering his prayer. One of his old ewes was going to give birth out of season, and from the size of her he guessed it might be twins. He brought her into the garage so he would be close by if she needed him. The twins were born one cold night. The first struggled quickly to its wobbly legs and began to nurse as soon as the ewe would let him. But when the second one, the runty one, tried to join her brother, he butted her away. The old ewe walked to the far side of the garage with her firstborn close behind. The little one just stood there bleating, too weak to follow.

Isaiah wrapped her in an old car robe and carried her to the warm kitchen. He always kept a baby bottle handy and he fetched it from the shelf. He had his head in the refrigerator getting out the milk when he heard Travis's bare feet pattering on the linoleum.

"What's the matter?" she asked sleepily.

He took out the milk and poured some into a saucepan, nodding as he did so at the blanket-wrapped lamb in the rocking chair. "It was twins, and the old ewe can't take care of both. So she sent this one over to you."

"To me?" Her eyes went wide.

"Yep. I'm fixing a bottle right now. Then you got to do it from now on. I'll feed her while you're at school, but I'm too busy to bother otherwise. You got to take care of her for me."

Travis walked over to the chair, from which came such piteous little bleats that Isaiah himself could hardly bear to listen. "Hush," she whispered. "Don't cry. Travis is going to take care of you."

Travis kept the lamb in a box in her room. They didn't tell Old Lettie it was in the house. It was their secret. At last they had something real to talk about, and Travis began to talk. She named the lamb Orphan Annie and fussed over it like a little old mother. To Isaiah's delight and relief, the lamb responded, growing strong and mischievous, like a young creature should. The man and the child never minded cleaning up after it. They scolded, of course, but instantly forgave. And Travis would immediately undo the effects of any scolding by petting and hugging and reassuring the lamb that they only spoke harshly because Old Lettie mustn't know, mustn't be upset.

The child was not only talking to him, she was smiling. Isaiah thanked the Lord every day for that mean old ewe and her troublesome lamb.

For Christmas he helped Travis buy a collar for the lamb. He also bought a little net stocking filled with chocolate candy covered with gold paper and a huge candy cane. Old Lettie had never celebrated Christmas in the years he had worked for her, so he could not count on her even remembering the date, and he wanted Travis to have something from Santa Claus.

After the Christmas Eve service at his church, which was near Bethel on the other side of the county, Isaiah always went on to spend Christmas with his old mother, so he took special pains to fix a nice dinner for the child on Christmas Eve. She helped him in every way she could, even getting the plastic flowers from the hall table to make a special centerpiece. He found some candles and lit them. Travis ran to switch off the ceiling light.

"My, that's pretty, ain't it?" he said.

In the candlelight her face seemed to glow. "You think Miss Lettie will like it?" she asked shyly.

"Sure to," he said, though he'd never known the old woman to like anything but a large profit. "Tell you what," he said. "I'll go up and make sure she comes down for supper tonight. You get Annie to the garage."

He found Old Lettie in her usual chair, not, for once, studying her books—just sitting there in the dark.

"Supper's ready, Miss Lettie," he said.

"I don't feel up to coming down."

"Just this once. It's Christmas and the child's got everything fixed up nice for you."

She had opened her mouth, probably to refuse, when it happened. There was a clatter and cry and crash after crash. Isaiah took the stairs five at a time, but it was too late. Their beautiful dinner was a jumble of broken china and glass all over the kitchen floor. Annie was standing there, the end of the tablecloth still in her tiny black mouth. Travis was holding the candles. "Nothing's on fire," she said and burst into tears.

"Now, now," he said. "It can't be all that bad." But when he pulled the light cord, it was hard to see how it might be worse.

He soon saw how. If the invitation had not brought Old Lettie down to join them, the sounds of disaster had.

"What's going on?" she cried. "What is that animal doing in my house? Wrecking everything I own?"

"Just go on back upstairs, Miss Lettie," Isaiah said.

"I'll get this cleaned up in no time. Travis, you best get the lamb outside."

"I don't know where that animal came from, but I know where it's going tomorrow!" the old woman shouted. "It's going to the slaughterhouse if I have to carry it there myself. What's going on in that head of yours, Isaiah? Letting that animal into my house. Hasn't my life been upset enough?"

Travis, her face white as the tablecloth, picked up the lamb. She staggered, adjusting to its weight. It was almost too heavy for her now. "Best take her to the barn," he said quietly under the old woman's raving.

"She can't kill Annie," the child whispered.

"Of course I can kill it. What do you think we raise sheep for around here, you foolish child? For slaughter—for market—so we can live."

Travis turned and stumbled out the back door with Annie in her arms. Isaiah let Lettie carry on while he cleaned the floor on his hands and knees. She would run down eventually. When she did, she fell exhausted into the rocking chair.

The kitchen was in order, but Travis had not come back in. The old woman was rocking agitatedly.

"I best go out and find the child." He was almost too angry with her to speak, and it was a struggle to keep his voice even. "If you get hungry, there's some cold cuts in the refrigerator."

He grabbed his jacket and flashlight and slammed out the back door. When there was no sign of Travis in the barn or shed, he went to the garage. He shone his flashlight on the old blanket in the back of the pickup. It had two humps under it, and one of them was wriggling, nervous as a snake. Isaiah hopped into the cab and started down the highway. After several miles, he heard a little tapping at the rear window of the cab. He looked into the mirror to see two noses pressed against the glass. He hoped he looked very surprised. At any rate, he stopped and ran around to the back to help his stowaways down. "Best come up front where it's warm," he said.

Travis, shivering like a newborn calf, didn't argue. She just climbed up on the seat, hugging Annie close.

He carefully shifted gears and pulled out into the road. "Where you two fixing to go?"

"Away."

"I see. Any particular place in mind?"

"California."

"Where your momma is?"

"I was only here temporary, you know. Just till she got settled."

"Sure."

"But I can't wait no more."

"Not like that man and his old poodle, huh?"

She didn't smile at his joke. "Lettie's too mean. How come my momma sent me to stay with somebody so mean and hateful?"

"I don't know," he said. He couldn't understand it himself. Couldn't Lucille remember why she ran away? "I guess she was kind of desperate. She figured Old Lettie for all her meanness would try to do her duty by you."

"I don't want to be her duty. It's miserable to be her duty."

He sighed. "Yeah, but you got to figure she's pretty miserable, too."

"Well, she can just be miserable all by herself. I'm not going to help her anymore."

He drove on for a while in silence, the headlights blinking up and down the bumpy road.

"Where you going?" she asked finally.

"Well, I'm due over to my church. All my relatives there give this big Christmas play and they're expecting me to join them. After that I'll go on into Bethel and say good-bye to my poor old momma. Then I'm fixing to run away, too."

"You can't do that!"

"Who says I can't?"

"Grown-ups don't run away. They go to California to find themselves."

"Well, I didn't know I was lost, but, whatever . . . Anyhow, since none of us is planning to go back there, why don't you come along with me—just for this evening?"

"They won't allow Annie in church."

"What d'you mean? That dumb sheep'll steal the show."

AND OF COURSE she did. Bethel Church had never had a live lamb abiding in the fields before. After the songs of men and angels and women and little children, the Angel Gabriel himself (who looked a lot like Isaiah Washington) told the shepherds (one of whom was female and dressed in a man's lumber jacket instead of a bathrobe) to get themselves over to Bethlehem and find that little baby boy lying in a manger and "take that no 'count little lamb along. If ever there was a sinful creature in need of God's salvation, she's the one."

The happy shepherds giggled, but they obeyed and took Annie all the way to Bethlehem to the feed box, in which lay Isaiah's grandnephew, Elroy, aged seven months. Annie went right over and began to nibble the straw, accidentally nuzzling the baby, who laughed out loud, which made everyone laugh and clap and burst joyfully into the final carol. Afterward they crowded around Travis and Isaiah and Annie to thank them for helping Bethel Church to have such a fine Christmas play.

Suddenly Travis had an idea. They would take the entire cast over to sing for Old Lettie. They would bring Bethlehem to her whether she wanted it or not. Isaiah wasn't sure it was such a good notion, and his relatives were even less sure, but Travis begged, and Annie let out the most pitiful bleat they ever heard in their lives. So they piled into cars and trucks and drove back across the county to the dark old house on the hill. They began singing along the road, and they were still singing when they got out at the house. They stood and sang on the sagging porch under the gingerbread trim, but there was no sign from the house that anyone was listening.

Travis ran to the door and *blam*med the heavy knocker with all her might.

"No, no," Old Lettie called out from just inside. "Don't come in. I don't want you to come in. Haven't

I been upset enough?" But Travis would not be stopped. She pulled the heavy door wide and ordered Isaiah and all the relatives and friends to follow her to the kitchen. Old Lettie trailed after them, sputtering like a faulty faucet.

Travis pushed her old aunt gently into the rocking chair beside the stove.

"Seems like we're going to do a little play for you, Miss Lettie," said Isaiah as he leaned down and put his laughing baby nephew into the old woman's lap.

She gave a little shriek. "Don't!"

"Careful!" Travis cried. "You'll drop the Baby Jesus!"

" 'There's a star in the east on Christmas morn!' " Isaiah's powerful baritone boomed out, and all the cast replied: " 'Rise up, shepherd, and follow!' "

" 'It will lead to the place where Christ was born,' " he sang. " 'Rise up, shepherd, and follow!' " they echoed.

Travis smiled and hugged her lamb, while tears poured down Old Lettie's face onto the child on her lap. And whether they were tears of anger or tears of joy didn't matter to Isaiah just then. It was Christmas. At least for this little while, heaven and nature were singing and all the lost lambs of the world had been found.

✳

Star Lady

ON THE FIRST morning of her retirement, Rosamund McCormick got up at a quarter to seven. There was so much to do. She would begin with the house.

The real estate agent had warned her that December was a terrible month to sell a house. Even in a good year, people didn't buy in the winter, he had said. But Rosamund hadn't gotten to be one of the state's "Outstanding Women of Business" by listening to other people whine. There were plenty of wealthy young couples on the lookout for a beautifully kept ninety-year-old house with hand-carved mantelpieces and hardwood floors.

The neighborhood was no longer a handicap, she

told herself over coffee. There had been a time when her son had urged her to move. Many of the older houses had deteriorated, and nearly everyone she knew had fled to the suburbs. The patrons at Miller's grocery store had changed first in color and then in language, and, sad to say, there was usually a wino or two hanging about the small parking lot.

Grace Church, in which Rosamund had been baptized and married, had changed, too. When dear Dr. Lancaster died, they called a bearded boy right out of seminary who spoke to God as though He were a fraternity brother. The educational building, named the Weatherford-McCormick Building for her husband and her father, was turned into a day care center. And the choir— She shuddered. The choir loft that had once resounded with Bach oratorios now yipped with discordant modern jingles. She blanched to recall one awful one in which the refrain had been "Hooray for Jesus! He's our man!" Rosamund refused to make a fuss. She quietly moved her membership to the large downtown First Church, where the choir all had trained voices and the Trinity was addressed with proper deference.

During those years when the neighborhood as well

as the church and the corner grocery were going downhill, Rosamund had held on to her house. She had lived in it all her life, and she was simply too busy to take on the task of moving. Her husband, who had come into the family department store business when they married, died three years after her father, so Rosamund had to take over.

Now the neighborhood was on the verge of becoming fashionable once more. It was the perfect time to sell—a good time to leave. She had nothing to keep her. The business was in capable hands, her son was dead. She paused to refill her cup. Gail had remarried, of course, in less than two years. And, as if Rosamund hadn't suffered enough, the children, James's children, her grandchildren, had been adopted by Gail's new husband. She hardly saw them anymore.

She had planned to begin with the attic and work down through the house, throwing away everything except the antiques. She felt a great need to strip away all the physical encumbrances of her life and start afresh. But in the attic there were old letters and pictures, a worn-out football jersey, a weight-lifting set. No, it was not a day for the attic. Besides, from the window she could tell it was going to be one of those wonderful, almost springlike December days. She would begin with the garden. Hard physical exercise was the thing she needed.

The only time Rosamund ever allowed herself to wear trousers was in the garden. She used an old pair that had been her husband's, adding one of his hunting shirts for warmth. She tied her hair up in a scarf and put on her sturdy gardening shoes and yellow gloves.

She was pruning a rose bush when she spied the child staring at her through the hedge. Since she was on her knees, they were almost at eye level, except that it wasn't his eyes that she noticed first but the red, very runny nose. The hedge—she must make a note to call the nursery on Monday—was a bit scraggly at that spot, and the boy was standing in the alley behind it, obviously watching her.

"May I ask what you want?"

"Hi," he said, almost at the same moment.

"What are you doing there?" She couldn't help feeling that he had invaded her privacy, if not her territory, as he elbowed his way through the hedge.

"Watch that hedge!"

"Don't worry. It don't scratch much."

"I didn't think it would hurt *you*." But the boy, who seemed to be about eight, wasn't listening. He was taking her measure with his eyes, looking at her yellow gloves, her oversized pants, her worn shirt, even the threadbare canvas pad on which she was kneeling.

"Ain't got no coat, I bet," he said sympathetically.

"Of course I have a coat. I'm just not wearing it at the moment."

He nodded, a smile lighting up his dirt-smeared features. "Sure, lady," he said. "I understand."

"Understand? Understand what?"

"It's tough, being winter and all. But I want you to know you got friends in this world."

Rosamund was too startled to reply. Where had this creature come from? As if in answer, he nodded south. "They explained everything to us in Sunday school. People need to know that God loves them and that they got friends in the world."

"Well, that's very nice. Thank you very much," said Rosamund in her briskest voice, the one that sent the most persistent sales representatives backing out of a room. The boy didn't notice. "Well, good-bye," she said loudly, rising and pulling off her scarf. She would try to finish the roses at a better time.

"White hair," the boy said. "You really are old. Wow."

"I am sixty-five," Rosamund said tightly. "Not dead yet."

"Sixty-five." His eyes, a sort of grayish blue, widened. "My grandma is only fifty. You're old enough to be my great-grandma."

"Hardly. Don't you have a tissue or something for that nose?"

"No'm." He snuffled noisily.

For an awful moment she thought he was going to wipe his nose with his hand. She turned away. "Well, good-bye," she said and began to hurry toward the back steps. He came trotting after.

"We're supposed to come in and give you Christmas cheer."

"Thank you just the same. I'm quite cheerful enough already."

He snuffled once more. "But," he said, "if I don't pay you a visit, I don't get a star. See, the team that gets the most stars . . ."

What idiotic nonsense! Still what could you expect from a church that sang "Hooray for Jesus?" "Oh, all right." She was trapped and she knew it. "Come on in—for a minute. I'm busy."

He followed so closely up the back stairs that she was afraid he would trip on the heels of her shoes, but somehow they made it to the porch. "Wipe your feet on the mat, please," she said, demonstrating. He nodded vigorously, elaborately smearing the garden mud from one end of the mat to the other, losing a bit on the porch in his enthusiasm.

At the door, she slipped out of her garden shoes and was walking stocking-footed over to the kitchen closet when she realized he had taken off his sneakers and was tiptoeing after her in gray socks that she imagined she could smell across the room. Never mind. She'd feed him and dispense with him in ten minutes flat.

"I suppose you'll want something to eat," she said as she put on her house shoes and stowed the garden shoes in the closet.

"Oh, no," he said piously. "It's against the rules to take people's food."

"And I suppose it's also against the rules to blow your nose?"

"I don't think so," he said. "Preacher didn't mention nothing about it." The back of the hand from which the sneakers dangled headed toward the nose.

"Wait," she said, diving into her purse, which lay on the kitchen counter. "I may have a tissue." But she came up with a handkerchief of Belgian linen and lace that she had bought on her world tour two years before. It couldn't be helped. She handed the handkerchief to the boy.

He took it without thanks and blew his nose loudly and wiped it with all the ceremony he had expended on the doormat minutes before. Then he held it out to her.

"No, no," she said. "You keep it. You might need it later."

He nodded and stuffed it into his jeans pocket.

"Well—" How was she to get rid of him? "Thank you for your visit."

But he was just then settling himself on the kitchen stool. "I guess you're all alone in the world. Got no one to spend Christmas with or anything."

She opened her mouth, but before she could protest, he went on. "No kids. Not even a job, I bet."

"If you don't mind . . ."

"My mom's got a job. She puts the little ones in the center. Works out real good."

"That's nice," Rosamund said tightly.

"Yeah. I didn't know how lucky we were." He smiled sweetly at her. "I was just this grabby little kid, thinking about what I was going to get for Christmas. Stuff like that."

"I see. Well, it's been nice visiting with you, uh—"

"Buddy," he said. "Name's Buddy."

She might have guessed. "Thank you, Buddy. Now. I'm very busy. I'm going to be moving soon and I have a lot to do."

"Moving? They gonna make you move?"

"Buddy, really, I must—"

"But miz—miz—that's terrible."

"Not your worry." She wasn't about to give the child her name or any more of her time. She swept him out the door, handing him his sneakers on the porch. He didn't seem offended and called out cheery greetings as he went, reminding her more than once that God loved her and that she was no longer friend-less. She smiled back primly, but the minute he was gone, she collapsed against the door, laughing until the tears rolled down her cheeks. She had to go poking about in her handbag for a tissue, which made her start laughing all over again.

She made a conscious effort to pull herself together. She was not going to become one of those old women who talk to themselves or laugh out loud in empty houses. But at the moment she couldn't think of any-one to call and tell. Her friends wouldn't be able to imagine how very comical it was—that solemn little runny-nosed boy bringing her Christmas cheer so his Sunday school team could get a star. And she had given him her Belgian linen handkerchief . . . James would have loved it. But James was dead and she hardly ever saw his wife or children anymore.

The laughter evaporated as she thought of her grandchildren, who were growing up without her. She had tried to visit, but Gail and she had never been close, and Gail's new husband seemed ill at ease in her presence. James's children, who had once been so tiny and dear, had suddenly become loud and unmannerly, eager to be off to some party or other. She had begun spending all her holidays in Florida. It was easier on everyone.

A FEW DAYS later, there was a note on her door when she got back from the hairdresser's. It was on lined notebook paper and clumsily decorated with crayoned stars and Christmas trees.

Dear friend (she could barely decipher the handwriting), this is to invite you to our Christmas Joy Service on Christmas Eve at 7 p.m. at

Grace Church. We want you to know that God loves you and you have lots of friends. There will be eats, too.

Your special friend,
Buddy Collins

P.S. Don't worry. You can wear your old clothes. It don't matter.

Christmas at Grace Church. She remembered all too well the last Christmas Eve service she had attended in Grace Church. There were at least eight different-colored electric flames in the windows. The minister paraded two dozen or more squawky-voiced little children to the front to sing some jangly tune . . . with rhythm instruments. Rosamund sighed. Tacky. That was the only word for it.

She allowed herself, just for a moment, to go back to the Christmas Eves years ago when the sanctuary had been dimly lit with a pair of standing candelabra among the poinsettias. Into the darkness and the hush, the choir, sounding like a single voice from the vestibule, began the ancient carol "Let all mortal flesh keep silence . . ." Then they walked in solemn procession down the main aisle, carrying candles, the haunting melody growing in power as they came, until at last they massed under the majestic pipes of the choir loft ablaze with light. The music soared, filling the church and reverberating from the great dark beams of the rafters:

"Alleluia, Alleluia, Alleluia, Lord most High!"

She shivered at the memory of it. The wonder and the power and the mystery. And now . . .

She balled up the grubby little note and dropped it into the hall basket.

But Buddy, as she found, was not to be dismissed so easily. Two days before Christmas, she was in the midst of decorating her tree when the doorbell rang.

"Hi," he said cheerfully.

"Oh, Buddy, I'm very busy right now. I'm decorating my Christmas tree."

"You got a tree?" He rushed by her at the door to come in for a look. "Oh." He sounded relieved. "It's real tiny." He went closer to the table on which the tree stood. "Not even real." This time his voice segued into its sorrowful key. "But it's nice." He looked up, his dirty little face radiating sincerity.

"Thank you, Buddy."

"It's real nice you keep trying. Some old people just give up."

"Do they, now."

"Yeah. You ought to see the ones over to the home. It's real pitiful—some of 'um don't even know who they are anymore."

"You'll be glad to know that I still know who I am."

"Good for you." He beamed, patting her arm. "You just keep it up." He picked up a glass ball from the box on the table and shook it.

"Buddy," she said as quietly as possible, "that ornament is nearly one hundred years old. Would you be kind enough to put that back into the box? Very carefully."

"Huh? Oh, sure." She watched, hardly breathing, as his hand, which was too big for his small body, lurched against the side of the box, rattling the delicately painted glass ball back into its place.

"Cost too much to get new ones these days, don't it?"

"Yes," she said, sighing with relief. "Well, Buddy, it was nice of you to come, but I am busy right now."

"I could help decorate your tree."

"No!" The word came out more sharply than she'd intended. "It's just that I'm getting ready to move and . . ."

"Oh, yeah." Sympathy poured through the dirt on

his face. "Oh, yeah. I almost forgot." He started backing toward the front door. "But don't you worry. Just remember—God loves you, and you got friends in this world."

"I won't forget, Buddy. Be sure your team gets another star."

He missed the irony, of course, beaming his most evangelical smile. That's who he reminded her of. Those television evangelists with their toothy smiles. Only their faces were cleaner.

SHE FORGOT ABOUT her little gospel bearer until the phone call early Christmas Eve morning.

"Rosamund? Merry Christmas! It's me, Gail."

"Yes, Gail." She could feel her body stiffening.

"It's been too long since we've seen you."

"Yes, well, I've been quite busy."

"We'd love to have you join us for dinner tomorrow."

"I have plans."

"I would have called you earlier, but I just assumed you'd be in Florida as usual."

"No. I'm moving down as soon as I sell the house. I felt the need to stay and get it ready."

Why was Gail laughing? Rosamund hadn't said anything funny. She'd never understood Gail. She felt the impulse to slam down the receiver but restrained herself. "Thank you for calling," she said crisply.

"No, no, no, wait—" Gail was trying to suppress her giggles. "I have to explain."

"Yes?" She was curious despite her annoyance.

"Peter called." Gail could only mean Peter Freedman, the new president of Weatherford Department Store, Inc. "Someone called the office to ask about you."

"About me?"

"Yes, apparently"—and here another giggle bubbled up—"apparently there is a rumor going around the neighborhood that you have lost all your money and are on the verge of eviction."

"Eviction?"

"I know it's crazy, but that's what the minister told Peter."

"What minister?" But she knew the answer. "That bearded boy at Grace Church?"

"That's the one."

"Buddy." Rosamund bit the name as though it were a profanity.

"Pardon?"

"I've got something I have to attend to, Gail. I'll talk to you later."

"About dinner. . ."

"Later." She clanged down the phone. That dirty-faced, runny-nosed busybody, making a fool of her at the church, at the company, even with Gail. Just because she'd tried to be nice.

She had a cup of tea to calm herself before calling the church office.

"Grace Church. God loves you, and you have friends in the world. Merry Christmas!"

"Yes. This is Rosamund Weatherford McCormick. I would like to speak to the pastor."

"He's not in right now. Can I take a message?"

She was delighted to note that all the bounce had seeped out of the secretary's voice. "In that case," she continued, carving each word out of ice, "I would like the telephone number of a child by the name of Buddy Collins. I understand he attends your Sunday school."

"Uh, Mrs. McCormick. Maybe you ought to speak to Bill first."

"Bill?"

"Reverend Farley."

"I thought you just said he wasn't in."

"He's not, but—"

"Then I will take the Collins's number."

"I think Reverend Farley wants to talk to you about a misunderstanding."

"The telephone number, if you please."

"I don't know if they have a phone. I don't seem to have a listing. . ."

She finally extracted the street address from the reluctant secretary. It was one of the tumbledown houses that backed hers on the alley. She went to her bedroom, carefully applied her makeup, and dressed in a soft wool peacock-blue dress, and—although it was totally inappropriate for morning wear—pinned a large diamond brooch at her throat. Then she put on her cashmere overcoat. If Buddy had difficulty identifying quality, his mother ought to be able to recognize that Buddy's Sunday school project was not teetering over the edge of either senility or poverty.

She stormed down the alley, around the corner, and up the street, looking for the proper number. She guessed the house before she got to it—one of the once handsome Victorian mansions that had been chopped into apartments. The grassless front yard was overrun with small children and dogs, all of which seemed to be wagging their tongues at her. In a tangle of frantic barks and high-pitched squeals—"Whatcha want, lady?

Whatcha want?"—she made her way through the yard to the front door. There was no bell, so she knocked loudly, nearly bruising her knuckles in the effort to make herself heard over the din.

At last someone came to the door. Buddy, carrying a baby almost as large and runny-nosed as himself.

"Oh." He cocked his head. "My mom's at work." And then suddenly, as though finally recognizing her above the cashmere collar and taking in the meaning of her visit, he hung his head. "Preacher told me you ain't being thrown out of your house."

"No," she said, her anger already evaporated.

"I ain't going to bother you anymore. Don't worry." He began to close the door with his foot, juggling the baby as he did so.

Just then a little girl who had been in the yard bumped past her and shoved the door wide open. "This your star lady, Buddy? The one you was telling about?"

"Shut up!"

"Is it? Is it?" She danced around, looking at Rosamund from every possible angle.

"No!" Buddy yelled. "You don't get no stars for bothering rich people. You just get stars for helping the poor and needy."

"You didn't get a star for me?" Rosamund asked.

"I got the wrong house," he said. "Supposed to see this old lady on welfare, and I got the wrong house. Preacher give me the devil for it, too."

Rosamund smiled despite herself. "We're going to get your star back," she said.

The boy sneaked a look and when he saw the smile, he smiled shyly back, shifting the squirming baby to his other hip.

"I don't care," he said. "It was dumb, anyway."

"But the preacher ought to know."

"Know what?" He snuffled.

"That . . . sometimes . . . rich old ladies need friends, too."

"Yeah?" He jiggled the baby to quiet it, his eyes on its almost hairless head. "Wanna come to church with me tonight?" he whispered.

"Of course," she said.

THE SANCTUARY WAS lit with the same garish electric candles, and the music, if anything, was worse than she had remembered. The congregation was a variegated mix of race and age.

In a specially designated front section, all the children in Buddy's Sunday school class were sitting with their star people. The children's beaming faces alternated with the tired faces of the neighborhood's aged outcasts. Rosamund was sure that the man two down from her was one of Miller's grocery store's winos, his breath coming down the pew sour and strong. On the other side of Buddy, a little girl, pink ribbons bouncing in her black plaits, was proudly arranging the crutches of her star lady under the pew in front.

Instead of the stately alleluias of bygone years, Rosamund could hear the cry of a sleepy baby in the rear, echoed by the hacking cough of an old man at the end of her row.

After an exuberant attack on "Hark! The Herald Angels Sing" that would have roused the dead to protest, the bearded young preacher read the Christmas story in a jarring modern version. "What is the message of Christmas?" he asked. "What does it mean to us that this baby was born in a barn all those years ago? Today, in Grace Church, when we hear this story, what does it make us want to say to our neighbors?"

"God loves you!" the children yelled. "And you got friends in the world!"

Buddy turned to her and smiled. His face, cleaner than she had ever seen it, reflected all the light in the sanctuary. "Me, too," he whispered hoarsely, patting her knee. "I got me a friend, too."

Tears started in her eyes. Suddenly she found herself snuffling. She began to poke into her purse but, before she could find a tissue, Buddy jabbed her arm. He was returning her handkerchief—clean, slightly gray, and very wrinkled, but obviously scrubbed.

She mouthed a thank-you and gently blew her nose. What would James have thought—Rosamund the star lady, sitting in the second pew with all the poor and needy of the neighborhood, blowing her nose. Or Gail? And the children? She couldn't wait to tell them tomorrow when she saw them.

A slightly different version of this story was published in The Virginian-Pilot, *December 24, 1982.*

Exultate Jubilate

CHRISTMAS IS OVER. Sally is putting the children to bed, and I am sitting in the living room staring at a rocking horse and trying to figure out what happened to me last night. You must understand, first of all, that I have always entertained a certain sympathy for Scrooge. There he was, going about his business as best he knew how while all around him the world was going mad. 'Tis the season to be jolly? Come, now. What is there to be jolly or merry or even mildly happy about? How can anyone who watches the evening news on a daily basis work up a case of holiday cheer? Frankly, I weary of Christmas carols that start jangling through the malls on Halloween. The decorations on the lampposts that the city fathers drag out every Friday after Thanksgiving have begun to show their age. And so have I.

My wife is another story. She goes into a frenzy of decorating and baking and, since August, has been in a panic trying to decide whether or not to give a present to the Steadmans. I just try to stay out of her way.

I want my kids to be happy, but it's hard to be patient when they pester me for months for junk they've seen advertised on TV that anyone over ten knows wouldn't last out the twelve days of Christmas. Can someone explain to me why, as the days grow shorter, the pitch of children's voices gets higher and higher? Besides, this year business has been, if not bad, certainly not robust, and I simply didn't have the money, not to mention energy and goodwill, to waste on the latest fad.

Still, the only reason I didn't go around literally grunting "Bah! Humbug!" this year was because of the kids. They are only three and six, and I am enough of a hypocrite not to try to ruin their excitement, much as my head aches to tone down the shrill. But somehow I drew the line at going to the Christmas Eve service last night. Once I slid out from under my mother's "Thou shalt nots," I became quite happily an Easter,

Christmas, and whenever-my-mother-was-visiting Christian. But this year even Christmas seemed too much.

I told my wife I would stay behind to organize the stocking gifts and put the rocking horse together. Every year it's two or three in the morning before we can get to bed. And then we're too angry with each other to sleep. The year of Mike's tricycle was a low point in Christmases past—one reason Jenny was getting a rocking horse.

"The children will be so disappointed if you don't come," she said.

"Oh, they don't really expect me to go to church."

"But it's snowing, and you know how I hate to drive in the snow."

"Why is it that I have three more years of payments on a certain four-wheel-drive Subaru Wagon?"

"But I don't like leaving you here all by yourself on Christmas Eve," she said. "You'll get gloomy and moody."

"In two hours," I whispered, lest any little ears be nearby, "I'll have that rocking horse put together, and all we'll have to do is stuff the stockings and dream of sugarplums." That cinched it. She remembered all too well the long night of the tricycle.

"Daddy isn't feeling up to church tonight," she told the children. I coughed obligingly and helped her zipper the snowsuits and yank on the boots, and happily waved them off to church.

A half hour later, I was not so happy. The rocking horse that I had so carefully purchased was proving to be, in my mother's picturesque phrase, "an instrument of the devil."

It was not on rockers, but attached to its stand by huge, coiled springs. I had, by the hardest effort, pulled three of the four springs and hooked them into the stand. But every time I got the fourth nearly in place —sweating and straining to make it stretch to the last eye—the spring would recoil viciously, gouging my flesh as it flew through my hand.

I was glumly staring into the living room fireplace with a large brandy in my hand when the doorbell rang. My impulse was to ignore it. Sally had the garage opener. She wouldn't be ringing the front doorbell, and nobody we knew would be dropping in for a visit. The bell rang twice before I roused myself, put down my drink, and shuffled to the door.

Through the peephole I could see a youngish-looking man. He was wearing a windbreaker, but his head and hands were bare. He was carrying a paste-board box and he looked frozen.

I opened the door about an inch. "Yes?"

He smiled. His lips were cracked and his nose and cheeks raw. "Would you like to buy some Christmas greens?"

The man had obviously not seen the inside of our house. "Sorry," I said, starting to close the door on his smile.

"Well, merry Christmas to you," he was saying when I remembered the stupid horse. Maybe the guy could help.

I opened the door wide. "Come in," I said with heartiness so false any fool would have suspected me of being up to no good. "Come in and get warm, at least. You must be frozen."

He put down his box of greens, stamped the snow off his thin shoes, and stepped in gratefully. "Not many sales tonight," he said. "I expect most people are all ready for Christmas."

"Yeah," I said. "Could I get you something hot? I think there's still some coffee."

"Gee," he said. "That's real nice of you." He fol-lowed me down the greenery-festooned hall to the kitchen. "Wow," he said, "you sure don't need more greens. You're loaded."

"My wife's a little bit crazy on the subject of Christmas," I said, pouring out a mug of coffee for each of us. "Milk and sugar?"

"If it's no trouble." He held the mug out for me to put in the milk and then the sugar, and then stick in a spoon. "Thank you," he said, stirring deliberately while he looked around our big kitchen. Sally had wreaths and ribbons even in there. His hands were so chapped they looked as though they'd been bleeding.

"Smells like Christmas," he said.

I hadn't noticed, but in addition to the evergreens the room was full of the warm odor of cinnamon and cloves and the Christmas bread that Sally had baked that afternoon.

"Nice, isn't it?" he said.

"Well, yes, I suppose so. If you like that sort of thing." My mind was on getting the horse done before Sally and the children got back, but I couldn't very well snatch the coffee I'd just given him from his hands.

"I guess you have a pretty tree, too."

Well, what could I do? He obviously wanted to see our tree. I led him back down the hall to the living room. Our house is not one of these energy-efficient moderns. It's Victorian with a fifteen-foot ceiling, and the tree scraped it. I think Sally picked out the house so she could have monster Christmas trees. There is certainly no other reason for a ceiling of that height. You should see our heating bill.

The visitor was standing there, his mouth open, his eyes shining like a three-year-old's. "That's the most beautiful tree I ever saw in my life," he whispered.

"Yes, well," I felt almost apologetic. "My wife—"

He turned, his face still full of awe. "She must be a wonderful person."

"As wives go . . ." I tried to joke, but it wasn't going to work. The guy was as sincere as a cocker spaniel. "Don't let your coffee get cold," I said.

He ducked his head and took a sip, but over the rim he was eyeing my sound system. Oh, dear. Maybe he was casing the joint. I took his elbow to steer him to the family room, where one three-legged rocking horse sat waiting, but he resisted me.

"I know I shouldn't ask you . . ." He smiled his childlike smile. It was impossible to believe that such a lovely smile, cracked lips and all, belonged to a potential thief. "I mean, you've been so nice, but I'm so hungry for real music. Just while I'm drinking your good coffee?"

He looked hungry for meat and potatoes, but how could I refuse such a request? "Okay," I said, "a bargain. You can choose any music in the cabinet if you'll help me put together a rocking horse for my daughter."

His smile broke into a laugh. "I'm getting the best end of that." He handed me his still almost-full cup and fairly ran to the cabinet.

While he fingered the CDs and tapes lovingly, I wondered what he might choose. There wasn't much there that would appeal to a person of his class. There were dozens of recordings of Christmas carols—even one, so help me, of those cartoon chipmunks singing traditional tunes.

"Here," he said, his eyes glowing. "This one, please."

"Are you sure?" He had handed me Mozart. The Colin Davis London Symphony recording of Mozart's sacred music. Now wouldn't you have been surprised?

"Do you mind?" he asked anxiously when he saw my hesitation.

"No, of course not," I said.

"I don't look like a Mozart lover, right?" His smile was on crooked now.

"Well, I mean . . ." There was no way of getting

out of that one. I put down the coffee cups and inserted the tape.

I waited for the great "Kyrie in D Minor" to boom out, and after adjusting the sound slightly, picked up the coffee cups and started for the family room and the horse.

"No!" He grabbed my wrist. Coffee sloshed into the saucers from both cups. "Listen."

"Kyrie Eleison!" the voices demanded. *Lord have mercy!* "Christe Eleison!" *Christ have mercy!* I thought I had heard it before, but I realized, as I looked at my visitor, that I had never really heard it. His eyes were closed. I felt distinctly uncomfortable. "Come on," I said, slipping my wrist out from under his hand, being careful to keep from spilling coffee on Sally's rug. "We've got to get that fool horse done before my family gets home."

He opened his eyes and looked at me. I thought he was going to object, but he grinned. "Yes," he said, "our bargain."

"It's in there, too." I jerked my head at the sound system. "The music goes all over the house."

"Oh," he breathed. "That's wonderful. You can live in music." He followed me to the den.

There sat, or should I say, sagged the horse with Mozart showering down upon its head. "If you pull that spring," I said, nodding at it with my head, "I'll try to yank this side in toward you so you can hook it."

He was listening to the Kyrie and not to me. I hated to interrupt him, but we did have this bargain. "The horse," I said with a bit more urgency in my voice. "They're likely to get home any minute . . ."

He nodded, but I knew he wasn't paying attention to me. I should have been angry, but somehow, he was forcing me to listen to the music, too. I handed him back his coffee. "Just through the Kyrie, all right?" I said. "Then we do the horse." I'm not sure if he heard, but he took the coffee and sat cross-legged on the floor, his head cocked toward the wall-mounted speaker.

I sat on the couch, watching him listen, but it was not a stranger's profile I was seeing but the face of my father singing this very Mozart one Christmastime when the civic chorus had decided against the usual *Messiah*. My father died when I was seventeen, so I must have been a young teenager.

I loved to watch my father sing. Of all the faces in the chorus, his was the one that appeared to be listening rather than showing off. He always seemed to believe the music that he sang. And although I was an arrogant kid full of questions and resisting any answers, I loved the humble reverence I saw in him. I never told him though. It wouldn't have been cool or neat or whatever our catchphrase was in those days. And then he died.

I went to the kitchen and cut a piece of Sally's Christmas bread and brought it to the stranger—to make up for never having told my father that I loved to watch him sing. "You're too kind," the young man murmured. Me, too kind? Lord have mercy, indeed.

How, I wondered, in some future Christmas would my children remember me? Certainly not as I remembered my father—his face glowing with the glory of the music he sang.

I could almost see a huge festive table with a grown-up Mike and Jenny and their families gathered around. And Sally, white and wrinkled, but still not a bad-looking woman. "I wish your father could be here today," she was saying.

"Dad?" Mike was frowning. "He'd hate it. I mean, the very fact that we are here would mean that civilization hadn't blown itself to bits. You know how he hated to be proved wrong about anything."

"Mike! What a thing to say!" Thatta girl, Sally.

"You remember the news bulletins?" Mike went on.

"Children"—now Jenny, my sweet little girl, has jumped into it—"children, the minute the tree went up your grandfather would begin reading aloud items from the newspaper to prove how awful the world was—that there was no peace, no goodwill, no hope, no joy—"

"Exultate Jubilate!" the choir sang out. With a chill of relief, I shook off the ghost of Christmas-yet-to-come and turned my attention again to my visitor. His face shone as his cracked lips moved, mouthing the Latin words of joy and exaltation. How could he, with raw face and chapped and bleeding hands, be joyful? How, in fact, could the starving Mozart have known such a moment of exquisite joy? How could a baby born in a barn bring such beauty, such glory into this greedy, self-destructive, cruel world?

Suddenly I heard the clatter of the garage door. I jumped from the couch. "They're back!"

"Oh." The young man hastily picked the crumbs of bread off his windbreaker and jeans and popped them into his mouth. He half rose. "I'm sorry," he said. "I was lost . . ."

"It's too late. I'll get them into the front room. You

just slip out when you can, and make sure the door is shut." He looked puzzled, maybe a little hurt. "The horse," I explained. "I don't want the children to see it." And I slammed the family room door on his confused and embarrassed face.

"What glorious music!" Sally said as I met them in the back hall. "It makes me feel like being jubilant." She's a beautiful woman, especially when she's happy. "I'm glad you've been listening to Mozart," she continued, taking off her hat and shaking out her lovely hair. "I rather pictured a different scenario. . ." She gave me a wry look.

"Okay," I said to the children. "Let's take all the boots and snowsuits off in the back hall."

"It's cold out here, Daddy," Mike started. "I want to take them off in the family room."

"Now, now," I said, "no complaints. Joy to the world, and all that!"

" 'Cause it's Christmas!" Jenny shrilled, but her voice didn't pierce through me as it had earlier.

"That's right," I said and bent down to help with her boots but kissed her cheek instead.

"You tickle!" she giggled and put her fat little arms around my neck. I bent closer to the boots, so she wouldn't see my eyes. I was feeling very rich.

We had our family time together before the living room fire. I never heard the stranger leave, but then it must have been sometime after the "Alleluia." I can't imagine he would have left before that heavenly "Alleluia."

"THIS HAS BEEN a lovely evening," Sally sighed as she tied the ribbon on the last package. "The nicest Christmas Eve I can remember."

"Yes," I said. "Thanks to you. Everything looks so beautiful and smells so good."

She laughed. "It's the same every year. I didn't think you noticed—except for the bills."

"Well, I noticed, and I like it."

"It was your music that did it for me," she said. "I wouldn't have thought of Mozart for Christmas Eve, but it's perfect. You have no idea how it felt to open the door and hear that magnificent 'Exultate' come pouring out." She smiled. "What a wonderful idea."

Then I remembered the horse and the stranger I'd left in the family room. "Oh, Sally," I said rushing down the hall. "I totally forgot . . ."

I opened the door. He was gone, of course. I think

I was relieved. I'm sure I wouldn't have known how to explain him.

Sally was behind me. "You did it," she exclaimed. "Good work." Then I realized that the horse was no longer sagging but stood upright, proudly stretched on all four legs—ready to gallop its way into Christmas morning. The stranger had kept his side of the bargain.

So here I sit trying to figure it all out. Who would believe that a man who is still closer kin to Scrooge than to Tiny Tim would, on a bleak midwinter night, be visited by an angel?

I think I'll go put on the Mozart.

The Handmaid
of the Lord

PEOPLE THINK WHEN your father is the minister that you get special favors, like you were God's pet or something. Rachel, for one, knew absolutely, positively that it was not true. God didn't love her better than Jason McMillan, who was getting an entire set of Mighty Morphin Power Rangers for Christmas. God didn't love her better than that Carrie Wilson, who was getting a new Barbie dollhouse with two new dolls, outfits included. Not that Rachel really wanted a Barbie dollhouse, or Power Rangers either, for that matter, but it was the principle of the thing. Carrie and Jason were getting what they asked Santa Claus for. When Rachel asked Santa for a horse, John and Beth just rolled their eyes. John and Beth were her older brother and sister. Beth was eleven and John, thirteen, and they thought they knew everything.

"But where would we keep a horse, Rachel?" her mother had asked. She was changing baby David's diapers and not paying Rachel much attention. "We live in the church manse. You know how small our yard is."

"Rachel," her father had said in his most patient voice, "what is Christmas really about? If all you think about is Santa Claus, you're going to miss the main event." Rachel's heart sank. When your father told you to think what Christmas was *really* about, she knew what that meant. It meant no horse. Not even a pony. Ministers' kids never got really good presents at Christmas. She should know that by now. It didn't count if you were naughty or nice. Gregory Austin had pulled the alarm last Sunday and made the fire trucks come in the middle of church service, but he was getting his own personal computer. His daddy had said so. Her daddy told everybody they were supposed to be God's servants. Like Jesus was. He didn't even mention presents.

So—no good presents. Rachel had given up on that. But a big role in the primary classes' Christmas play—that shouldn't be too much to ask for. She was by far the best actress in the second grade. *Plus* she went to Sunday school every single week, even when she had the sniffles, or it snowed so hard that she and John and Beth were the only kids there.

"Don't you think a kid who comes every single Sunday no matter if it's a blizzard should get a good part in the primary classes' play?" she asked.

"We live next door to the church, stupid," John had said. "You don't get brownie points for walking across your side yard."

"You're the minister's daughter, Rachel," Beth had said. "It would look bad if you grabbed a big part."

"You got to be Angel Gabriel in both the second *and* third grade," Rachel reminded her.

"That was different," Beth said. "I was the only one in either class who could remember all the lines. The head angel has a lot to say. Besides I speak out. Everyone in the back row heard me perfectly."

"I can speak out," Rachel said, but no one paid any attention.

When she was five, she had been part of the heavenly host. It was a terrible part. The angel costumes were made of a stiff gauzy stuff that itched something awful. Afterward Mrs. MacLaughlin, who ran the pageant, yelled at her right in front of everybody.

"Rachel Thompson! Angels are spiritual beings! They do not scratch themselves while they sing! You had the congregation laughing at the heavenly host. I was mortified."

Last year Mrs. MacLaughlin had taken a rest from directing, and Ms. Westford had run the pageant. Ms. Westford believed in equal opportunity, so for the first time in the history of First Presbyterian Church, girls had been shepherds and wise men. That was okay with the girls, but the boys were mad. They didn't like the itchy angel costumes at all. And a *lot* of the fathers complained.

But Rachel had been a much better shepherd than those stupid boys. She didn't care what anyone had said afterward. She knew what the Bible meant when it said the shepherds were "sore afraid." When Mr. Nelson shined the spotlight at them to show that the angel of the Lord was about to come upon them, Rachel had shown everyone in the church what it meant to be "sore afraid."

"Help! Help!" she'd cried loud enough to be heard by the people in the very back row. "Don't let it get me!"

The congregation laughed. So did Gabriel and all the shepherds and the entire heavenly host. Mary laughed so hard she started choking, and Joseph had to whack her on the back.

Her father said later that it had been "a brand-new insight on the Christmas story," and her mother said, "Never mind, dear, they weren't laughing at you." But she knew better. No one in the whole church understood what the story was really about. When the Bible said "sore afraid," you were supposed to be scared. When that big light hit her face, Rachel had been trembly all over. She knew in her heart that she was the only kid in the pageant who felt that way. Not even the second- and third-graders who got all the big parts did them right. If you couldn't have a scratching angel, you sure shouldn't have a Joseph yawning so wide you could drive a tractor trailer straight down to his tonsils.

It had been a hard year. Her mother had been tired and pregnant for most of it, and then when David finally was born she'd gotten tired and busy. Beth thought David was the "cutest thing in the world."

"Was I cute when I was little?" Rachel asked her.

"I can't remember," Beth said. "I know you cried

a lot. And your face got really red." And she went back to goo-gooing at the baby.

John wasn't as silly, but he was always bragging about how great it was to have a little brother *finally*.

"What's the matter with little sisters?" Rachel asked. John just rolled his eyes.

Now at the end of the worst year of her entire life, Christmas wasn't going to be any better. Even the carols were against her. All those songs about the City of David. "Couldn't we make up a Christmas song about the City of Rachel?" she asked her mother. But her mother just smiled and kept on singing about David.

"Hey," John said one night, "I just realized. We're all in the Christmas story—David, Elizabeth, John—"

"What about me?" Rachel said.

"Oh, you're in it," John said.

"I am?"

"Yeah. I can't remember the verse, but there's something off the side of the story about somebody named Rachel weeping and wailing."

"It's because King Herod killed all her children," Beth said.

It wasn't fair. Everyone else had a nice place in the story—everyone but Rachel. It made her more determined than ever to have a good part in the play, one in which she would not scratch or yell or wail. Mary. She would be Mary. She was old enough this year. She was the best actress in the second grade. Surely, even if she was the minister's daughter, Mrs. MacLaughlin would pick her. She'd be so good in class that Mrs. MacLaughlin would just see that nobody deserved to be Mary more than Rachel did.

Besides, her little brother had already been chosen to be Baby Jesus. She ought to be Mary. Jesus shouldn't have a stranger be his mother. It might scare him.

"Now," said Mrs. MacLaughlin at the first practice. "It's a good thing we have a lot of kindergarten to third-graders in this church because we have a lot of parts in this play."

"Mrs. MacLaughlin?" Rachel said.

"What is it, Rachel?" Mrs. MacLaughlin's voice sounded a tiny bit impatient, so Rachel talked fast.

"I know I'm the minister's kid and that when I was little, sometimes—"

"Yes, Rachel—"

"Well, I've studied the part really hard, and since my brother is the Baby Jesus, I thought, well, it would probably mean a lot to *him* if—well, if his big sister could be Mary."

"But we don't have sixth-graders in the play, Rachel. Elizabeth's too old."

"I don't mean Elizabeth, Mrs. MacLaughlin. I mean, well, what's the matter with me?"

There was a burst of laughter in the room. Everyone was laughing at her! Rachel's face went scarlet. "Shut up!" she yelled. "I'm serious. I know the story better than anybody here, and it's my brother!" Everyone laughed harder. Even the little ones who were going to be itchy angels were giggling.

"Rachel—dear—" said Mrs. MacLaughlin after she finally got control of the group. "Of course you know the Christmas story—after all, your father is our minister—but—but Mary is a very difficult role."

"I could do it," Rachel muttered, but she knew it was no use. People weren't supposed to laugh at Mary. And everybody laughed at her—when they paid her any attention at all.

"Carrie," Mrs. MacLaughlin was saying. "How would you like to be our Mary this year?"

Carrie Wilson? She had blue eyes and blond curls all the way down her back and didn't look at all like Mary. And that fake smile. It made Rachel sick to her stomach. Carrie Wilson's Mary would look like a plastic wimp. Mary was the handmaid of the

Lord, for heaven's sake, not some department-store dummy.

Rachel could hardly listen as Mrs. MacLaughlin went down the list telling everyone what they were supposed to be. She knew now she wouldn't even get a speaking part. Mrs. MacLaughlin didn't like her. Nobody liked her. Not even God. Finally, Mrs. MacLaughlin stopped.

Rachel looked up. She hadn't heard her name. She didn't want to say anything because maybe her name had been called when she wasn't listening and then Mrs. MacLaughlin would have something else to fuss about. But she couldn't stand it. She raised her hand.

"Yes, Rachel?"

"About my part—"

"Yes, Rachel. This year you have a *very* important part."

"I do?"

"Yes. You will be our understudy."

"Our what?"

"Since you know the story *so* well, you will be prepared to *substitute* in case any of our actors become ill or unable to perform."

"Substitute? You mean I don't have a part of my own?"

"You have *all* the parts—in case— Why suppose, for example, Gabriel should lose her voice? You would step in and be our Gabriel."

Jennifer Rouse, the third-grader who had been chosen to be Gabriel, gave Rachel a dirty look. She had no intention of losing her voice. "Or if"—here Mrs. MacLaughlin smiled sadly at Carrie Wilson—"our Mary were to suddenly have to visit her grandmother in Ohio, you would have to step in and be our Mary."

"My grandmother's coming *here* for Christmas, Mrs. MacLaughlin," Carrie said sweetly. Rachel wasn't stupid. She knew what Mrs. MacLaughlin was doing. She wasn't keeping Rachel from having a big part. She was making sure that Rachel wouldn't have any part at all.

SHE TOLD HER MOTHER that she was never going back to Sunday school again in her whole entire life. "Nonsense, dear," her mother said. And, of course, she went back. Ministers' children have to go to Sunday school. It's the law or something.

And then, a miracle happened. One week before Christmas, Carrie Wilson, who wore the world's prissiest little blue leather boots, slipped on the ice in the mall parking lot and broke both her arms. *Both* her arms. Rachel was overcome with exceeding great joy. God did love her. He did! One arm might count as an accident, but two arms were a miracle. God meant business. No matter how determined Mrs. Mac-Laughlin was to keep her out of the play, God was going to make sure not only that she got in but that she got the most important part in the whole shebang. She was going to be Mary, the handmaid of the Lord.

Of course, she didn't tell anybody how joyful she was. She was too smart for that. When Mrs. Mac-Laughlin called her on the phone, Rachel practically cried at the news that she would have to pinch-hit for our poor little Carrie. "I'll do my best, Mrs. Mac-Laughlin," she said quietly and humbly, just like the real Mary would have.

She went early to the dress rehearsal so Mrs. MacLaughlin could try the costume on her. It fit perfectly. Well, it would have fit practically anybody. Those robe things weren't exactly any size, but Rachel took it as a good sign when Mrs. MacLaughlin sighed and admitted that, yes, it did fit.

"Don't you worry, Mrs. MacLaughlin," Rachel said. "I'm the understudy. I know the part perfectly." Which was a little silly since Mary didn't say a word, just looked lovingly into the manger while everyone else sang and carried on. But she wanted Mrs. MacLaughlin to know she wasn't going to do anything to make anybody laugh this year. She would be such a good Mary that Mrs. MacLaughlin would be practically down on her knees begging her to take the part again next year. They'd probably have to extend the play past third grade so that they could keep Rachel in the role of Mary until she was grown up and through college and had babies of her own.

"We have to eat early," she told her mother on Christmas Eve. "Mrs. MacLaughlin wants the cast there an hour before the service."

"Thank goodness," said John. "I don't think I could stand another hour of loud glorias sung off-key."

But Rachel didn't care. She was so happy, the glorias just burst from her. Besides, she had to get them all out before seven o'clock. She couldn't let a stray gloria pass her lips when she was behind that manger. God might understand, but Mrs. MacLaughlin sure wouldn't.

She was all dressed in the sky-blue robe, sitting quietly, looking down into the empty manger. Mrs. MacLaughlin, hoarse from yelling at the heavenly hosts, was giving last-minute directions to the wise men, when suddenly the back door of the sanctuary opened.

"Why, Mrs. Wilson. Carrie—" Mrs. MacLaughlin said.

Rachel jerked up in alarm. It *was* Carrie, standing in the darkened sanctuary, her fake-fur-trimmed coat hanging off her shoulders, both arms bound to the front of her body.

"She insisted," Mrs. Wilson was saying. "She said, 'The show must go on.' I talked to Dr. Franklin, and he said it would be the best thing in the world for her. She was so distressed about letting everyone down that it was having a negative effect on the healing process—"

Two mothers yanked the beautiful blue robe off Rachel and draped it over Carrie's head. "See. It was meant to be," Mrs. Wilson said. "It totally hides the casts."

Rachel slunk off the platform and slumped down in the first pew. No one noticed. All the adults were oohing and ahing about how brave Carrie was to come and save the play.

"Oh, yes, she's in terrible pain," her mother was saying. "But she couldn't bear to disappoint you all."

No one cared that Rachel was disappointed. Not even God. Of course, God had known all along that

Carrie would show up at the last minute and steal back the part. God knew everything, and he had let Rachel sing and rejoice and think for a few days that he was on her side, that he had chosen her, like Mary, to be his handmaid. But it was just a big joke. A big, mean joke. She kicked the red carpet at her feet.

"Off stage, off stage, everyone. Time to line up in your places."

Where did you go when there wasn't any place for you? She looked around. People were beginning to arrive for the service. She slipped farther down in the pew. She didn't want her family to see her. They'd find out soon enough that God had fired her.

She saw her mother carry David up the far aisle. The baby was sucking happily on his pacifier. He would be a good Jesus. Everyone would say so. Mrs. MacLaughlin was waiting at the door to the hall. She took David and said something to Mom, who cocked her head in a doubtful manner. Was she telling Mom that Rachel wasn't going to be Mary after all? If she did, maybe Mom would come over and take her on her lap and tell her she was sorry. No, Mom didn't even look her way.

The play went well. None of the angels cried or scratched. Gabriel knew all her lines and said them loud enough to be heard almost to the back row. The wise men remembered to carry in their gifts and nobody's crown rolled off. Joseph did not yawn, and Mary gazed sweetly into the manger. It was all perfect. Perfect without her. Rachel felt like weeping and wailing like the Rachel in the Bible.

And then, suddenly, a miracle occurred. Baby Jesus began to cry. Not just cry, *scream*. Yell his little lungs out. Carrie Wilson forgot about being Mary. She turned absolutely white, and her eyes went huge, like she was about to panic. She would have probably got up and run, but with her arms bound under her robe she couldn't move. She looked at Joseph. "Do something!" she whispered. Joseph's face went bright red, but he didn't move a muscle.

It was all up to Rachel. She jumped from her pew and dashed up the chancel steps. She was still panting when she got to the manger. Rachel poked around under the baby until she located the pacifier and jammed it into David's open mouth. He clamped down on it at once. The big church went silent except for his noisy sucking. Rachel smiled down at him. He was a lovely Jesus.

"Who do you think you are?" Carrie Wilson hissed through her teeth. But the whisper was almost loud enough to be heard in the back row. Rachel could hear a snicker from somewhere out in the darkened sanctuary.

"Behold." Rachel straightened up and stared sternly in the direction of the offender. There was no doubt that the people in the last pew could hear her. "I am the handmaid of the Lord! And I say unto you, glory to God in the highest and on earth peace and goodwill to men, women, and children."

Nobody laughed. They didn't dare.

About the Author

Katherine Paterson was born in China, the daughter of missionary parents. Educated in both China and the United States, she graduated from King College in Bristol, Tennessee, and received a master's degree from the Presbyterian School of Christian Education in Richmond, Virginia. After studying and working in Japan for four years, she was awarded a fellowship to Union Theological Seminary in New York City, where she met her husband, the Reverend John B. Paterson. The Patersons have four grown children and two grandchildren and live in Barre, Vermont.

A two-time recipient of both the Newbery Medal and National Book Award for her novels, Katherine

Paterson has also published essays and written a book in collaboration with her husband. A previous collection of Christmas stories, *Angels and Other Strangers*, was published by Crowell (now HarperCollins) in 1979.